Richard Carpenter's

ROBIN OF
SHERWOOD

THE BLOOD THAT BINDS

I0618621

Richard Carpenter's
Robin of Sherwood
The Blood That Binds
By Iain Meadows
Adapted by
Barnaby Eaton-Jones
Published in 2025 by
Chinbeard Books

in association with
Oak Tree Books
oaktreebooks.uk

Editor: Barnaby Eaton-Jones
Sub Editor: Harriet Whitehouse

Richard Carpenter's

ROBIN OF SHERWOOD

THE BLOOD THAT BINDS

by
Iain Meadows

Adapted by **Barnaby Eaton-Jones**

A Chinbeard Books / Oak Tree Books Original

Richard Carpenter's

ROBIN OF SHERWOOD

THE BLOOD THAT BINDS

by

Iain Meadows

PROLOGUE

The blond-haired young man, his tall powerful frame tense, his handsome features etched with concern, was looking at his 'father'. Not his biological father, but the man, the spirit, who had summoned him all those months ago to be his son and take up the mantle of the 'Hooded Man'. Robert of Huntingdon had become Robin Hood.

As he looked at Herne the Hunter, he had no idea of what to expect from the vision the older man was experiencing. Inside the cave that Herne inhabited, the fire that burned within the brazier had brought the trance to the point of fruition.

The weathered, rugged face of the Lord of the Trees was lined and tanned from his years of living at one with Sherwood forest; it looked on in concentration. Almost imperceptibly, his lips started to form words.

'The moment draws close when the hooded man must face those who command the powers of darkness,' he whispered. 'They who have sown the earth will face the reaping. It is the time of the harvest.'

'I will stand firm,' Robin replied. 'The people will not starve. Nor will they have empty purses. I swear it.'

'There is more,' Herne intoned. 'A destiny awaits you. It would see you save one who is bound to you by blood, and is yet a stranger to you, divided from you by that same blood.'

Robin considered these new words. 'That sounds as if there's no choice in the matter,' he said, glumly.

Herne's reply was unequivocal, 'If you value those close to you, there is not.'

'Unless I take a new path. A man may choose where to tread.' Robin countered.

'Perhaps. But if that were true, you would not be here,' was the Spirit Lord's reply.

Again, Robin considered. Then, with a slight frown, he told Herne that he would be careful where he walked. With that said, Robin left the domain of spirits, and their pronouncements of how life might be, and headed out into the world of harsh realities.

After he had gone, Herne—disentangling himself from the vision world—looked deep into the flickering flames of the fire and softly reminded his absent son of one inescapable fact. His voice was a low mumble.

'Once before you tried to run and could not! So must it be, Robin i' the Hood…'

CHAPTER ONE

Robert De Rainault, the Lord High Sheriff of Nottingham, looked disdainfully around him. With such immaculate and fastidious attention to his appearance, he found the whole process of strapping on his chain mail armour, and escorting taxes, a chore.

Sir Guy of Gisburne however, riding next to him, felt the opposite. The young knight, with his floppy curtains of blond hair, stared arrogantly ahead, never happier than when he was in the saddle.

It was as the two men were escorting this particular wagon through Sherwood that the outlaws struck. Despite the fact that the Sheriff had anticipated that something might happen, and despite the fact that Sir Guy had brought a considerable amount of soldiers with him, when the attack came it spread chaos through the ranks.

Will Scarlet, the most vengeful of Robin's men, and Nasir—the efficient Arab warrior—were managing to make it look like they were ten men instead of two. Turning their attention onto the wagon, the drovers, urging their horses forwards, found they were separated from their escort as they raced off down the forest track. Now it was up to Scarlet and Nasir to keep the soldiers at bay whilst the others went to work.

Robin leapt onto the passing wagon. He was aided by Little John, the giant of a man, who—to begin with—had had a wary relationship with the successor to Robin of Loxley. Now though, the two were close friends and a highly effective team. They quickly subdued the drovers and brought the transport to a stop.

Marion, with her long auburn hair flowing freely, ran quickly to the cart. In one smooth movement, her lithe body had leapt on board and she had brought her bow up, ready to cover the track from any counterattack.

She was joined immediately by Much, the miller's son. Since the death of his brother, Robin of Loxley, he had grown up considerably. He was

5

no longer a simple youth but a young man who was capable and ready to fend off any assailants. He had also—like Little John—taken well to Robert of Huntingdon as their new leader.

What Marion and Much saw, however, was no counterattack but the ample figure of Friar Tuck, hurrying down the track towards them, huffing and puffing.

'Come on!' urged John, and with good reason. The Sheriff, Gisburne, and what remained of their men were riding at speed towards the wagon. Scarlet and Nasir had done all they could before making their escape.

'Warn them off, Marion!' cried Robin as he sat ready to spur the horses into action once Tuck joined them. Marion loosed her arrow, quickly nocking another into place.

Finally Tuck reached them, and with considerable grappling and complaining from Little John about how much the friar weighed, he was dragged on board.

As Robin spurred the horses on, the wagon began to move. Marion fired again. Much also let loose with his sling shot and the most amazing thing happened—the shot found the Sheriff! His horse now reared up, unseating De Rainault from his saddle, sending him crashing to the ground. His helmet, coming off as he fell, meant that his head hit the floor with a firm thud.

The last thing the outlaws saw were Gisburne and the men-at-arms pulling up their horses, in order to attend to their fallen Lord.

'Did you see that?' asked an incredulous Much. 'I shot the Sheriff! I didn't have time to shoot Gisburne too, though.'

'The devil's own luck!' said John, as they rumbled on.

At the exact moment the outlaws launched their attack, miles away within an underground chamber inside his castle, Lord William de Baucher was in communion with a force that was beyond this world.

His thin, wiry frame was taut and his grizzled face, with his dark thinning hair swept back off it, was wrapped in concentration. Through the powers of this entity with which he communed, he had seen the events that had just been unfolding within Sherwood. When Much had loosed his sling shot, it was this unholy alliance that had guided the projectile to hit the Sheriff. Now, as he heard the voice of Little John joking with the young man about having the "devil's luck", he let out a low laugh.

'No, not the *devil's* luck, outlaw; something even greater. A power that only the chosen can understand!' he said, before exalting, 'Oh King of the world, what is your command, my master?'

'The time draws near.' replied a disembodied voice that resembled de Baucher's own. 'He will summon us. You must be ready.'

William de Baucher bowed. Everything was prepared.

Sir Guy of Gisburne was off of his horse and at the unconscious Sheriff's side. With all the subtlety of a man who believed that every situation required a show of force, Gisburne was now yelling at his Lord and master in an attempt to rouse him.

The Sheriff groaned as he began to come round. 'What happened?' he asked.

'The halfwit used his sling shot. It was a lucky blow. You fell from your horse, my lord, and hit your head.' Sir Guy was feeling a surge of pleasure at the Sheriff's lack of horsemanship.

'And what are you *doing*, Gisburne?' asked the Sheriff, scorn dripping from his words.

'My first duty is to you, my lord, so I ceased the pursuit to make sure you were unharmed.'

'Wrong!' snapped back the Sheriff, explosively. 'Your *first* duty is to make sure that the taxes currently being stolen don't end up deep within Sherwood, you prize-winning buffoon! Resume the pursuit at once!'

'My lord! But, what about you?'

'I can see myself back to Nottingham, Gisburne. I'm not devoid of a sense of direction…' he watched as Gisburne and the men mounted their horses, and began to gallop off, 'unlike you!' he added, 'They went THAT way, you dolt!'

Gisburne quickly reined in his black mount, gestured to the remaining soldiers, and they turned back to gallop off in the right direction this time.

The Sheriff tutted as they passed him, rolling his eyes so hard that they disappeared briefly behind his eyelids.

By the time De Rainault reached the village of Wellow, it was late afternoon and he was not feeling well. His head was pounding and the nausea he was experiencing—as the world seemed to spin all around him—was so bad, he knew he must stop and rest.

Shouting for the headman to show himself, a grubby, thin, middle-aged individual came shuffling out from one of the ramshackle huts, and made his way over to where the Sheriff was dismounting from his horse.

'My lord Sheriff, you are welcome.' said the headman.

'I doubt that,' replied De Rainault. 'It's Geoffrey, isn't it?'

The headman was a little taken aback that his name had been remembered. 'Geoffrey, it is, my lord. What a fine memory you have.'

'And what a fine bit of grovelling you're doing. Now, what I need is less flattery and more a place to rest, Geoffrey.'

Confused and a little alarmed at this turn of events, Geoffrey asked, 'You mean here, my lord? In Wellow?'

'Of course here!' snapped the Sheriff. 'Why am I always surrounded by imbeciles?' he muttered, as his head swam.

With little in the way of pleasing accommodation to offer, Geoffrey had no choice but to show his lord to his own quarters.

The hut's fetid atmosphere hit the Sheriff as soon as Geoffrey opened the door and showed him in.

The head woman, Jude, was busy over a cooking pot. Unaware of their guest, she was unguarded when she muttered to who she thought was just Geoffrey, 'What rotten luck, eh? The worm of a sheriff shows up here today, when we have the last of the venison to finish. Luckily, he'll never find it!'

'Venison, is it?' said De Rainault, 'Then we'll have to call it a last supper, won't we.'

Jude now flashed her husband a look of fear, realising that she had just signed both their death warrants. For his part, De Rainault had to lie down before he collapsed. Geoffrey quickly led the Sheriff to a pile of straw. 'This is what passes for your bed?' he sneered, 'I ought to have you flogged for this alone. As it is, we'll talk about that other matter once I've rested.'

Geoffrey helped the Sheriff onto the bed; he closed his eyes and instantly feel asleep. His heavy breathing and snoring filled the little hut.

Geoffrey turned on his wife—as she was

expecting him to do—and hissed, 'Why couldn't you keep your mouth shut, Jude?'

'I didn't know you were going to bring him in here, did I? Whatever possessed you?'

'You think I had a choice, woman?'

It was then that a dark thought crossed Jude's mind. She moved closer to her husband, and spoke in his ear, 'What if the Sheriff was dead?'

'But he's not, he's just sleeping,' responded Geoffrey, not catching on.

'What if he were accidentally smothered in his sleep, though?' continued Jude, 'Nobody would miss him, would they?'

Geoffrey looked at her in shock. 'So, instead of the possibility of just us hanging for the venison, you're now suggesting every single person in Wellow should die alongside us because the Sheriff was murdered in our village? What fumes have you been inhaling over that cooking pot?'

Jude countered, 'Not if we moved the body out into Sherwood.'

'And then we'd be damned for all eternity,' said Geoffrey, 'De Rainault's spirit wouldn't rest, we'd never be rid of him. I can't send a man to his maker.'

Jude looked at the Sheriff, in his deep slumber. 'Yet, when that evil worm wakes up, he won't think twice about sending both of us to meet the almighty at the end of a rope. Think on that, husband.'

CHAPTER TWO

It was first light when De Rainault woke to the sound of the cock crowing, and it took him a moment to get his bearings.

He sat up and noted that his head had now, thankfully, stopped throbbing. From outside the hut, he could hear the sounds of the village of Wellow already at work.

Stepping outside and stretching his aching muscles, he spotted Geoffrey, the headman—who had seen him immediately too—as he came shuffling over at speed.

The Sheriff breathed in the warm morning air. It seemed like it could well be another fine day. 'We have unfinished business,' he reminded his host, before adding, 'Let me tell you what's going to happen. In return for your hospitality, I am willing to overlook certain things.'

Geoffrey fell to his knees, thanking the Sheriff profusely, but De Rainault hadn't finished. 'There is that matter of that filthy straw on which I had to sleep.'

Geoffrey wondered what punishment was to be handed down and prepared for the worst.

'You obviously need new supplies,' said De Rainault. 'Take these coins and buy whatever you need, with my thanks.'

De Rainault had pressed two gold marks into Geoffrey's hand before Geoffrey could quite register what was happening. He looked warily at the small fortune he was holding. 'Are you feeling quite well, my lord?' he asked nervously.

'Like a new man,' came the reply. The Sheriff suddenly became aware of two villagers arguing. 'What's going in there?' he asked. The headman, desperate to see the nobleman on his way, assured him that it was nothing. De Rainault, though, was walking over to the rowing women, hastily followed by his host.

As soon as Rosie, one of the arguing villagers, saw the Sheriff, she bowed, before then accusing her neighbour, Liza, of stealing her bread.

De Rainault looked Liza straight in the eye and asked her whether she had indeed been a thief. Liza, shamefaced, crumbled under the Sheriff's gaze and confessed that she was guilty.

De Rainault now delivered his judgement, 'You shall both share the bread. Further, since the village is obviously in need of help, I give you my purse.'

There were audible gasps from the villagers at the sight of the Sheriff handing a leather purse to their headman.

Geoffrey was stunned as well, especially after receiving the coins a mere few seconds ago, but not too stunned to realise that if he didn't say something, then this gesture could easily turn sour. 'Hooray for the Sheriff!' he cried.

As the villagers cheered, as much in fear as in delight, the Sheriff's horse was brought over. He mounted up and was about to go, when he looked at Geoffrey. 'You didn't think I was going to go before mentioning the venison, did you?'

The villagers stopped mid-cheering.

'No, my lord. I guess I didn't. But honestly, it had nothing to do with my wife. She just said some silly words when you arrived. It is I who should be punished. *I* am the one who is guilty,' Geoffrey proclaimed.

De Rainault looked at the village. 'You're all guilty!' he proclaimed, and every heart in every villager sank to the pit of their stomach. He then added, 'Guilty of being hungry, of course. We all need to eat, Geoffrey. Good hunting!'

And with that, as the villagers started to tentatively cheer him once again, De Rainault turned his horse in the direction of Nottingham and rode out of Wellow.

Deep in Sherwood, the outlaws had just finished listening to Geoffrey recount what had happened with the Sheriff the previous day in Wellow.

Now, with the day drawing on, the headman started to say his goodbyes.

Robin reached for a bag of money, 'As the Sheriff seems to be in such a giving mood, here's something else from him, your tax monies back.'

'Oh,' said Geoffrey, almost embarrassed, before going on, 'You see, the thing is, we don't really need it. Give it to the poor.'

And with that, he was on his way.

'Did you hear that?' asked Little John, as soon

as Geoffrey was out of earshot. 'The poor. Give it to the poor. He *is* the poor.'

'Not anymore he's not,' replied Marion, 'Not for the moment, anyway. Did you see the new clothes he had on? Understated, yes, but those weren't clothes made by himself or the villagers. Those were bought from somewhere else or made by someone else.'

There was silence in the camp, as they processed the oddity of Geoffrey's sudden wealth. The fact that the wealth had been achieved merely through the Sheriff's kindness was even more astonishing and unbelievable.

It was Will Scarlet who raised a thought from the silence, 'What if Geoffrey 'as been turned?'

'Become an informant for the Sheriff, you mean?' asked Robin, ruminating.

'Nah,' said John, 'Someone would have told us if that were the case.'

'Besides,' noted Tuck. 'Geoffrey seemed as surprised as we were.'

'So, what was the Sheriff up to?' asked Marion, giving voice to the question they'd all been thinking about.

'Maybe he really is kind now?' Much suggested, ever eager to see the good in people rather than the bad.

'He doesn't know how to be,' countered Marion, well aware of the man's scheming, unethical, and greedy ways, when she was living at Nottingham castle under his care. How long ago that seemed now, when she first gave up luxury and warmth for the squalor and cold, all for the love of one idealistic rebel. An idealistic rebel who'd got himself killed, and now she'd fallen for his blond-haired successor. Her feelings, of late, had been a mix of loyalty to her new love and a desire to take a break from it all, to be able to think clearly again.

'And yet, something has changed,' said Nasir, in his clipped tones; talking about the Sheriff but, for a second, it seemed to Marion as if he was reading her mind.

They all looked at Robin. 'I don't know why you're all looking at me?' he countered, almost laughing. 'You all know Nasir's right. Something has changed. We just need to find out what has caused it.'

In the Great Hall of Nottingham, a roaring fire burned in the hearth, even though the day outside was warm. The cold seeped into the stone walls and seemed to stay there, regardless of the sun's attempts to heat the mammoth structure.

All morning, the Sheriff had been listening intently to various petitions, until a sudden interruption from his deputy, Sir Guy of Gisburne, upset the order. A faint murmur rippled around the crowd as two peasants were marched with force through the throng, in the custody of the tall, young knight with the strikingly blond-hair and arrogant bearing.

Perhaps the situation genuinely does warrant Gisburne barging to the front of the queue, the Sheriff thought, *I'll pause proceedings so he can speak.*

'These are peasants from Rufford, my lord Sheriff. Guilty of not paying their taxes or providing for the tithe.'

If true, then this was a serious matter, but, as he looked at them, De Rainault just felt a pang of sorry instead of anger. The man and woman brought before him were painfully thin, caked in grime, and dressed in tattered rags. They were wearing their poverty.

'We have nothing to give, my lord,' they pleaded. 'It's been a bad harvest for us. Begging your mercy, it's not that we don't want to pay or provide for the church…' they trailed off.

20

'It's just that you can't,' finished the Sheriff.

'Or won't,' Gisburne interjected, cruelly.

'Sir Guy is right to point out that some people, who are less civic-minded than the rest of us, do try to avoid their dues. And for those people there can be no charity. Isn't that right, Gisburne?'

At this response, a cruel smile spread across the young knight's face. The Sheriff clearly had more to say, and this would usually be the part where he tore them down a strip with his wicked, razor-sharp tongue. Gisburne decided he could listen patiently, as he was always happier when the Sheriff's vitriol wasn't directed at him, for once. It would also make the end punishment much more satisfying, to first see these peasants belittled and mocked before the sentence was handed out.

'Life can be harsh,' began the Sheriff, and then deviated into rhetoric that Gisburne never expected to hear from the lips of the Lord High Sheriff of Nottingham. 'But I can see that you have faced genuine hardship,' he said, with a caring tone. 'Charity begins at home and so I am, therefore, exempting you from your obligations.'

Gisburne's smile didn't so much slowly evaporate as instantly vanish. He must have misheard the Sheriff, surely?

The peasants were bowing for all they were worth, slightly confused by this act of kindness, and thanking the Sheriff for his mercy.

De Rainault was about to deliver another shock to the two bowing, grateful wretches before him, and to Gisburne as well. 'Why don't you stop off at the castle kitchens on your way out of here, and procure yourselves some food?' he kindly suggested.

Gisburne exploded in anger. This was a step too far. 'I must protest, my lord!' he exclaimed. The Sheriff stopped and looked at the knight.

'You're right!' he said. 'Of course, Gisburne. What was I thinking?'

Gisburne sighed inwardly, it had obviously been a little jest on the part of the Sheriff and he was now bringing it to an end.

De Rainault continued, 'You shouldn't be benefitting from our kitchens,' he said, correcting himself as Gisburne's smirk returned to his gloating face. 'No, the whole *village* should benefit!' he announced. 'Sir Guy will escort you to the stores where you will gather all that you need.'

Again, Gisburne found himself burning up with rage. 'My lord,' he cried, 'you can't…' He didn't finish, as the Sheriff interrupted him.

'I know it's only a small gesture, and I know

that we're favouring one village over others, Sir Guy, but we do have a castle to feed as well. Now, see these good people safely back to Rufford.' De Rainault then turned his attention back to the list of petitioners.

CHAPTER THREE

>>————————→

It was a few nights later that the Sheriff's brother, Abbot Hugo, joined him, and Gisburne, for dinner in the Great Hall. Wearing a perpetual frown, the Abbot ate in silence, as did Sir Guy. Robert De Rainault couldn't help but notice how cold the proceedings were.

'I think we shall need more than the fire to warm us tonight,' he finally said, jokingly. 'You're both very subdued. Is the wine not to your liking, Hugo?'

'The wine is excellent,' his brother replied, and then turned the compliment into a complaint. 'It must have been quite costly, Robert.'

'It's only money, Hugo!' replied the Sheriff, happily, 'What do you think, Gisburne?'

'Pardon my bluntness, my lord, but I think we shall be lucky to even afford the rot they are obliged to cook in the kitchens now, at the rate we're going. The treasury, and the larder, is empty.'

Hugo stopped eating mid-mouthful. 'What do you mean, empty?' he snapped.

'Didn't you know, my lord Abbot? It's empty,' he said, his reply surly.

'Don't be so ridiculous,' Hugo countered, not quite believing his ears.

'It is the truth.'

'The larder and the treasury?'

'The tithes are also uncollected,' added Gisburne, heaping more bad news on the Abbot.

Hugo, finding it hard to grasp that the castle coffers, and—more importantly—the Church coffers, might actually be empty, asked why the tithes were not where they should be?

'I am under orders.' Gisburne's reply was short and to the point.

The Abbot now looked across at his brother, who was smiling. But it wasn't a mocking smile or a sneering grin, it seemed to be a happy smile of contentment. 'Robert, is this true? Does this have something to do with Robin Hood? What plan have you cooked up now?'

The Sheriff finished a mouthful of the roast boar they were consuming. 'It's quite simple, Hugo,' he said, 'You've more than enough crops in your stores.'

'You see?' said Gisburne.

The Sheriff sighed. 'The people should be able to eat, Gisburne.'

Hugo erupted. 'I need to eat, Robert, I need to eat!' he shouted. 'This is outrageous. Gisburne, tomorrow under my authority as Abbot, you will go out and collect what is rightfully mine... er... that is to say, the Church's. You will put the fear of God back into people!'

The Sheriff banged his fist onto the table. 'Gisburne, you will do no such thing.' He turned on his kin, 'My dear brother, Gisburne's methods are too brutal and what did that achieve? Nothing. The populace hate us.'

Hugo looked stunned. 'So what?' he yelped. He peered at his brother across the table, 'Are you blind drunk?'

'On the contrary,' came the reply, 'I've had the blinkers lifted from my eyes; I'm the most clear-headed I have ever been.' He paused, as if for dramatic effect. 'Gisburne! You are confined to the castle.'

'Seriously, Robert. How much have you had?' asked Hugo, still clearly in shock.

'Enough to know that I'm fed up with you always telling me how I should run things. I am the Lord High Sheriff, and I will do with the shire as I see fit. You will leave in the morning for the Abbey. Do I make myself clear, Hugo?'

De Rainault excused himself and made to retire to bed. As he did, the Abbot also rose from his place and followed his brother, imploring him to sober up.

Watching the two quarrelling men depart, Gisburne poured himself another goblet of wine. The situation was getting out of hand.

It had to be stopped.

The following morning, the outlaws had all split up to visit the Sherwood villages. As Robin and Marion approached the bridge that led into Wickham, they were sure that if anyone had heard what the Sheriff was up to, it would be their friend Edward, the headman of the village.

As they walked, they saw a figure running towards them. A diminutive, pretty-faced, young lady, with fringed brown hair and a wide-eyed innocence about her. Dressed as she was, it took them a while to realise that it was Meg, Little John's partner.

'Is John with you?' she asked excitedly when she reached them. 'Do you think he'll like my new dress?'

'I'm afraid John isn't with us today,' said Marion, 'But, my goodness, I'm sure he would approve of that dress, Meg. You look beautiful.'

Meg grinned and spun round, holding out the folds, to make sure they could see it in full. She was grinning from ear to ear. Her new dress looked expensive, but both Robin and Marion were keen not to jump to any conclusions.

'Do you know where we might find Edward?'

'Of course! Follow me,' she said, and she took them to where Edward was working, renewing the thatch on the main village barn.

Edward saw them approach, waved, and climbed down off his wooden ladder to greet them warmly. 'Robin! Marion! What can I do for you today?' he asked, his smile appearing from under his fair beard. He brushed back the straw-coloured hair that was adorning his head in the same way as the thatch was on the barn; thick, dense, and in need of attention.

'Edward,' began Robin, 'It's not what you can do for us, it's what we can do for you,' he added. Marion took a heavy bag of coins from her satchel and offered it to Edward. 'A gift from the Sheriff,' she said, 'In the form of your taxes being returned.'

Instead of accepting the money with his usual gratitude, Edward looked at it rather awkwardly. Marion cradled the bag, feeling a bit uncomfortable that he hadn't taken their offering.

'Meg's been showing us her new dress,' Marion said.

Edward seeming to take this is a slight, rather than an observation. 'Nothing wrong in having a new dress,' he snapped, 'People have a right to new clothes, every once in a while.'

'Neither of us would disagree with that,' Robin replied gently, 'We've been in the same attire for longer than we'd like.'

Edward sniffed, 'Well, why don't you use that money to buy Marion a new dress? That way, you won't worry about Meg's.'

This was most unlike Edward, his prickly nature being the opposite of what his normal attitude towards the outlaws was. As headman of Wickham, he'd sheltered, supported, and helped them many times, all with good grace and good humour.

Marion was worried. 'Is everything quite alright, Edward?' she asked, with genuine concern.

'Why wouldn't it be?' Edward replied, curtly.

'You seem a little… well… defensive, is all,' Robin explained, looking Edward in the eyes.

Edward's defensiveness crumbled under Robin's searching gaze, and his face changed from an annoyed frown to an open worry. 'I'm sorry. Things have been… um… I'm not sure how to put it? Things have been… strange, of late. I assumed you might have..?' he tailed off, not finishing the sentence.

'You assumed we might have what, exactly?' Robin probed.

Meg, who had remained silent up until this point, couldn't hold her tongue still any longer. She was somewhat of a chatterbox by nature. 'Edward, tell them. They clearly don't know. Go on, tell them just *how* strange.'

Wickham's normally jovial headman sighed heavily. 'I'd heard the stories,' he said, 'we all had, but I just thought it was wild talk. I mean, it seemed impossible to believe.'

Meg, frustrated at Edward dancing around the issue, blurted it all out. 'The impossible became possible, though! The Sheriff himself arrived in Wickham the other day.'

'Why didn't I know about this?' interrupted Robin, knowing that any visit from De Rainault was not going to be a pleasant one. 'I wasn't told. I'm sorry. How can we help? What has he done?'

'Done?' replied Meg. 'Well, that's just it. He didn't do anything... not really.'

'You're not making any sense. He must have done something?' Robin replied.

'I don't think you'll believe it,' said Edward.

'Try me!' said Robin, starting to get a little frustrated by Edward and Meg skirting round the issue.

'He gave me a new dress!' exclaimed Meg, 'This new dress I'm wearing. The Sheriff gave it to me. He said he'd been concerned when I presented the taxes to him for Edward, in the Great Hall, and had vowed to come to Wickham with a new dress for me.'

Both Robin and Marion were alarmed and instantly suspicious.

'Why would he do such a thing?' Marion wondered, to Robin rather than Edward and Meg.

'And he handed me a bag of money,' added Edward, 'so that the village didn't have to starve. He knew how short we were on food.'

Edward paused, as he saw the puzzlement etched across the faces of the visitors. 'I'm afraid I have as little idea why as you probably do,' before adding, 'all I know is that the stories of the same type of thing happening in the many villages of Sherwood seem to be true, if this gesture is anything to go by.'

Robin seemed to be struck dumb, his impassive face framed by his sun-bleached fair hair, his mouth partially open as he took in the news.

'I knew you wouldn't believe it,' Edward said. 'I mean, who would?'

Robin regained his composure. 'Of course I believe you, Edward,' he assured Wickham's leader, 'I just don't understand the method behind the Sheriff's madness.'

'So, you see,' said Edward, leaning against the ladder at the side of the barn, 'I just can't take the money that you're kindly offering. It would be better if you held on to it, for another time when we're more in need of it, maybe? Because, right now, Wickham has plenty to go round.'

'You understand, don't you?' said Meg, 'We're helping *you* this time!'

'Look, I'd love to discuss it further but—as you can see—the skies are blackening for a storm, and I need to get the thatching finished,' Edward explained, already beginning to climb the ladder back to the barn's roof.

As he climbed his ladder, Meg started to leave too, speaking over her shoulder as she went. 'I have to go too, but you'll both tell John that he needs to come see me soon, won't you?'

'We will, of course,' Marion replied, watching her skip away, swishing her dress from side-to-side.

'Don't tell him about the dress, I want it to be a surprise!' she shouted.

Robin shouted up to Edward, 'If you need us, Edward, you know where we are.'

Edward raised his hand in acknowledgement and smiled at them both.

Marion slipped the bag of coins back into her satchel, and she followed Robin out of Wickham. She was the first to break the silence they'd fallen into, as they crossed the little bridge on the perimeter of the village. 'Maybe Will was right. Maybe people *are* turning.'

Robin shrugged it off. 'Edward? Meg? No, I don't believe that,' he said, but he sounded unsure. 'But, whatever is going on, it doesn't seem to be doing anyone any harm... yet. Quite the opposite, I guess.'

'That's the problem, though, isn't it?' added Marion, 'It all seems too good to be true.'

Robin nodded in agreement, as they walked on.

CHAPTER FOUR

When Robin and Marion reached their camp, they found the others were already back and had plans for the remaining day, as the loud snores coming from Tuck made clear.

Marion found a patch of sun that was breaking through the trees and made herself comfortable in the grass. Robin was at a loss, still mulling over what had happened in Wickham, and almost snapped at Marion. 'Do you really intend to just lie there in the sunshine?'

Marion, shielding her eyes, looked up at Robin. 'Well, why shouldn't I? As Edward pointed out, there's a storm brewing and I want to enjoy the sun whilst it shines. Tuck's clearly got the right idea, relaxing away there. We don't get the opportunity often and, clearly, our normal help is not needed right now.'

'Relaxation,' said Robin, 'is not something we should indulge in. Not when we have tax money to give back to the people of Sherwood.'

'It didn't work in Wickham and, I'm sure, if you ask, everyone here will say that the villages they visited didn't need or want that money either.' She was being logical and pragmatic, rather than stubborn and awkward, but Robin felt he was being challenged.

'Aye, it were the same in Rufford,' said Little John, overhearing the conversation. He had a makeshift fishing rod in his hand, evidently intent on spending a day by the river.

'You're sure about that?' asked Robin. 'They weren't under any duress?'

'No. They're very happy… and had plenty of money,' John replied.

Robin now looked at Nasir who was sitting silently against a nearby tree, sharpening one of his blades. 'Nasir, what about Edwinstowe?' he asked.

'The same,' Nasir replied, with his usual paucity of words.

'What are we going to do with the taxes we reclaimed, then?' The question had come from

Much, who had wandered over to where Marion was lay and plonked himself down beside her.

'Well, we can't keep it!' Robin replied, his frustration showing.

'Look, Robin,' said Little John, 'All of this... it seems to be for the best, doesn't it? It seems like we've won. Maybe you should enjoy it?'

Robin looked around at them all. Tuck was fast asleep. Much, Nasir and Marion were enjoying the sun, John was whistling happily as he left camp to go fishing, and Scarlet—who had placed himself away from the group—looked like he was about to follow John. All of this calmness happening around him when he felt like they should be preparing for the moment that Sheriff finally sprang the trap he was so obviously laying. *Why can't they see it? Why are they being so foolish?*

Robin still had not lost the petulance that came with his youth and his nobility, and it was rising to the surface now. What made him a natural leader also sometimes made him so very single-minded. Whereas his predecessor was hot-headed with enthusiasm and passion, there was a quiet and reserved coolness running throughout the outlaws' second leader to wear Herne's bestowed cowl. He internalised, rather than externalised, his strength.

36

With a final glance around, he stormed out of the camp.

In the wake of Robin's departure, Much turned his head to Marion, as they lay by each other in the grass. 'I bet he'll be in a right mood with you later, Marion!' he noted.

Marion nodded and smiled, before replying, 'I think you might be right, Much. But he'll get over it. He's probably gone to cool off. It's too nice a day to fret.'

The gates of the inner courtyard to Nottingham castle opened quickly, allowing the black leather-clad rider through.

William de Baucher dismounted from his horse and was greeted by Sir Guy, who embraced his old friend. 'Thank you for coming at short notice.'

'How could I not respond to your summons?' De Baucher replied. 'By the sounds of things, we will have something better than the tourney to give us our sport.'

Gisburne smiled, remembering their many medieval jousts against each other, their rivalry on horseback never spilling off into real life, where they remained friends. 'I could not think of anyone else I would trust when it came to trying to sort this mess out,' Gisburne confided.

'This moment has been fated,' said De Baucher with an intensity that almost frightened Sir Guy. 'Have we not spoken about how *we* would run things if we were in charge? Now it seems it is necessary that we step in. That is why you have written to me.'

Suddenly, the same intensity that had scared him a moment ago, now seemed to seize Gisburne. He felt it take hold of him with a rush of hot blood, which translated into him talking at speed. 'Authority is collapsing here. Where once De Rainault ruled with an iron fist, he now oversees the shire with a limp wrist. His benevolence in his actions and his manner have all but stripped any vestiges of fear from the people we are supposed to command. Strong leadership is the only course of action now, to bring the people back into line.'

'I assure you, Sir Guy, this *will* happen.'

Sir Guy was about to lead his friend to the great hall, when he was taken by the arm in a firm grip. De Baucher quietly informed Gisburne that his men would be here soon. He made it clear that the castle guard were to place themselves under the authority of his captain.

'There isn't any need for that, surely?' Gisburne questioned. 'Those men are loyal to me, and I am loyal to you, as your friend, William.'

'Of course,' De Baucher replied. 'But, even so, a strong chain of command leaves no room for doubting where authority ultimately lies. Isn't this just what you have been talking about?'

'Yes, but I would like control of my own men,' Gisburne persisted.

De Baucher looked at him with a steely stare. 'Sir Guy. You summoned me here to help rebuild order. To do that, I need men around me that I can trust without question. My own men. If you are not with me in all aspects I demand, then I will have to assume that you are against me.'

Again, De Baucher's intensity scared the young knight before seeming to infect him once more. Before he knew what he was doing, Gisburne had acquiesced.

De Baucher had one more command. 'I think, as well, from now on, you should not be so informal. From this point, it is necessary that you address me as "My lord", as I address my master when in his presence.'

'Master?' asked Gisburne.

'Are we not all vassals to the Kings we serve?' De Baucher replied.

'Yes, of course, you're right... My lord,' said Gisburne, slipping back into the subservient role that he had been stuck in a rut with before the Sheriff had turned nice.

De Baucher relaxed his grip on the young man's arm and indicated that he should lead the way to the great hall of the castle.

The Sheriff looked up from the piles of paperwork that surrounded him on the high table. He rose and bowed politely to De Baucher, as Gisburne introduced him, before coming down the steps from the raised daïs.

'Had I known that Sir Guy was expecting a guest, I would have had a special dinner prepared. Perhaps I can get the kitchen to rustle something up?'

De Baucher returned the small bow. 'That will not be necessary. I am sure you have other things to occupy your time.'

The Sheriff raised a quizzical eyebrow and was about to say something when the doors to the hall burst open, and an outraged Abbot Hugo came striding in. 'What is the meaning of this, Robert?' he bellowed, almost tripping over his purple robes as he strode in, 'First you dismiss me and now you summon me, like some kind of servant!'

'But surely, my lord Abbot, that is exactly what you are?' said De Baucher, as Hugo finally reached them.

The Abbot, now noticing that his brother had company, was unaccustomed to this kind of rebuke, 'I beg your pardon?' he said.

'And I grant it,' De Baucher replied, before going on. 'You are a servant of... God, no?'

Hugo didn't bother to answer the question but instead turned to his brother, demanding to know who was daring to be this impertinent?

'This is Baron William De Baucher,' De Rainault explained. 'As for what you're doing here, I thought I made my position clear.'

It was then that De Baucher again stepped in to shed some light on the situation. 'If I might explain,' he said, 'It was I who summoned you, Abbot.'

Hugo was now very puzzled indeed. 'Why has a man I have never met before today, taken the liberty of summoning me to Nottingham, in the name of my brother?'

'Because, as a servant of the Lord,' De Baucher replied, 'Your charity and compassion will be needed, in what will be a difficult time going forward.'

Again, Hugo was flummoxed by this mysterious baron, who stood so stoically in front of him. 'What, in God's name, are you talking about?' he spluttered.

De Baucher now poured himself some wine before, in a matter-of-fact voice, explaining, 'The handover of power to me. That is what I am talking about.'

'What an absurd notion!' scoffed the Sheriff. De Baucher now turned on him, the flash of intensity back.

'I will tell you what is absurd,' he said, with a firm edge. 'A Sheriff who is not collecting the tithes, *that* is absurd, and who presides over empty coffers. Is that not true?'

'It is, my lord,' Gisburne chimed in.

This earned a sharp rebuke from the Abbot as he explained that his brother was clearly working to a plan. He then turned to the Sheriff and demanded that he reveal it, the time for being coy having passed.

'Very well. It's simple,' De Rainault said, 'The

plan is this: a happy society is one that benefits all. There's plenty for everyone.'

Hugo couldn't help but outwardly groan.

De Baucher had all he needed. 'Sir Guy's concerns were fully justified,' he said. 'The Sheriff has, indeed, taken leave of his senses; perhaps as a result of the recent fall from his horse that Sir Guy mentioned to me, whilst engaging outlaws in Sherwood?'

The Baron addressed the Abbot directly. 'You will remove your unfit brother from office,' he ordered. 'You can take care of him at the Abbey.'

Before Hugo, or the Sheriff, could formulate a reply, De Baucher had called forward two guards. Two guards who, the Abbot noticed, wore De Baucher's crest.

A brief scuffle ensued, where the wriggling De Rainault brothers were manhandled by De Baucher's men, and they were unceremoniously dragged towards the doors of the hall.

As they were being removed, Hugo ranted at Sir Guy, 'Gisburne, this is an illegal act, not sanctioned by the King! He shall be hearing of this!'

The Sheriff's steward smiled. 'By all means, my lord,' he replied. 'Tell the King of your brother's mismanagement. I dare you. You'll be the first with an invitation to the execution.'

And then, the De Rainault brothers were gone, as the doors slammed shut.

De Baucher now walked up onto the daïs and sat himself in the Sheriff's seat. 'Tomorrow, Guy,' he said, 'with the new dawn upon us, we will ride out and remind the people that hard work under strict rules brings peace to their pitiful lives.'

CHAPTER FIVE

It was another beautiful day. Again, the outlaws were at rest. Even Robin—after he'd had time to blow off steam—had to concede that, for the moment, the people of Sherwood were prosperous and happy.

However, all that was about to change as Nasir ran into the camp with the news that Gisburne was in Wellow. Sleepily, Will Scarlet said, 'That's nice, what's he doing?'

'He is being Gisburne,' Nasir replied. This was what Robin had both been afraid of and waiting for.

The outlaws began to scramble for their weapons and, in Little John's case, his shirt. It was as he was searching for it, that Scarlet asked if 'it' hurt? John was at a loss as to what Will was referring to.

Scarlet stepped forward and slapped him on the back, exclaiming 'Your sunburn!'

As John growled at the stinging pain, he went for Scarlet, who, dodged, evaded and accused John of not being able to take a joke.

Robin, witnessing the chaos, shouted at them to stop, with a steel in his voice that scrubbed out the humour of the bickering camaraderie that Scarlet and John shared.

As the outlaws began to calm down, Robin noticed that Marion wasn't with them. 'Where's Marion?' he asked, looking around again.

'She's at the riverbank, having a swim,' Much said, 'She said she wanted to cool off.'

As Robin picked up Albion, the sword of the Hooded Man, and put it into its scabbard, he turned to his men. 'Pull yourselves together. I want you ready to go by the time I get back from fetching Marion.'

It was as he was leaving that he shouted back, 'Oh, and someone needs to wake Tuck!'

Scarlet and John both looked at each other and then scrambled to see who could get to the cold broth first, in order to pour a bowlful over Tuck's head, anointing his monk's patch.

Robin wasn't long gone before he heard the

spluttering yelps of Tuck, rudely awoken from his slumber.

Wellow was in chaos, as the villagers were being terrorised and their huts ransacked. In the maelstrom of the chaos was Gisburne, marching around the village and barking commands to his soldiers. He dropped a few purses of money into one of the wagons he'd brought along.

'Leave no stone unturned, men! No nook or cranny untouched! We'll take crops, we'll take livestock, we'll take the monies we're owed.' He paused, and laughed cruelly, before adding, 'This is *harvest* time, after all!'

Geoffrey, the headman, ran over to the knight and threw himself on his knees, grabbing hold of Sir Guy's surcoat. 'Have mercy, my lord,' he implored, 'Leave us with something!'

'Oh, I will!' Gisburne replied. 'I'll leave you with the lesson of what happens to those who steal from their masters. I'll start with taking back the shirt you stole from my back.'

Gisburne had now grabbed Geoffrey and was

roughly attempting to rip the clothes from his body. The headman fought back. 'These clothes were bought with the money from the Sheriff, they aren't yours. He told me to use the money to buy new clothes! I did it on *his* orders!'

'The Sheriff's lost his reason! And *I'm* ordering you to return them to me!' Gisburne shouted.

Geoffrey would not, however, relinquish his newly-bout attire without a struggle. Gisburne, drawing his knife, plunged it deep into his side and the struggle ended. As the head of the village fell to the muddy ground, Gisburne sneered at his shocked expression, 'You miserable peasant, keep your rags; you'll need them to soak up the blood!'

As Geoffrey lay dying, an arrow came flying into the village, embedding itself into one of the soldier's wagons. Close behind it, bows raised, the outlaws emerged from the trees. The commotion in the village began to die down, as a stand-off began.

Robin called out, as they got closer.

'Gisburne!' he yelled, 'Tell your men to drop their weapons and move away from the carts.'

'And why would I do that, wolfshead?' Gisburne shouted back.

'Because you know what will happen if you don't,' Robin replied, as they finally reached the soldiers.

Gisburne looked with contempt at the outlaw leader. 'I don't take orders from you,' he spat.

It was then that Robin became aware of another figure, one clad in black leather, with a heavy velvet riding cloak, calmly emerging from one of the nearby huts. The man showed no fear as he finished a mouthful of apple, tossing the fruit to one side. 'Sir Guy is absolutely right,' he said, 'He doesn't take orders from you. He takes them from *me*.'

'And who are you?' Robin demanded to know.

'Baron William De Baucher!' came the reply. 'And there's no need to introduce yourself. You're the infamous Robin Hood, of whom so many serfs tell proud stories. It is an honour. But, I tell you what, as this is our first meeting, I will allow you to honour *me* instead by dropping your weapons and surrendering.'

Robin looked at the icy cool figure in front of them.

'If you've heard the stories,' he said, 'you'll know what I am capable of.'

De Baucher's reply was bold. 'All of England has heard these stories, but I think you may need reminding that new stories get written all the time. Like the one *I* am currently composing.'

As De Baucher moved his hands into the folds of

his cloak, no one saw the gestures he made; magical symbols traced into the air.

At that moment, mounted soldiers came charging into the village in a flanking move. Their speed, magically enhanced beyond all earthly possibilities, was terrifying. They were on the outlaws before they had properly registered their arrival. Too late—and in too close quarters to use their bows to any effect—the outlaws drew their blades and readied their quarterstaves.

Thus began a desperate fight against the supercharged troops, who rode at them time and time again.

'Everyone break!' ordered Robin, 'Try and make for the trees. GO!'

The outlaws scrambled as best they could, to get to the safety of Sherwood with the Baron's men-at-arms pursuing them.

Heading for the forest, the outlaws now found themselves accidentally split into two groups.

Robin, Little John and Nasir had managed to get their backs to the forest. They were almost into the relative safety of the trees when they spotted that Scarlet, Tuck, Much and Marion had all been cornered, their only choice being to surrender.

Robin made a move to help them but both Nasir and Little John pulled him back into the forest. 'We go, Robin!' Nasir said urgently.

'I'm not going without them!' Robin exclaimed. Again, he made to scramble back out of cover but was pulled back harder this time by the brute strength of Little John.

'We can't help *anyone* unless we're free,' he stated, calming his resistant friend. Both Nasir and John were of the same mind. Marion—above all of them—would always be Robin's weak spot, but if they were to mount any kind of rescue and save their friends, they needed to be free to regroup and find a better way to do so.

In the battle's aftermath, with the villagers cowering, De Baucher walked over to where the defiant quartet of Scarlet, Tuck, Much and Marion stood. He turned to Gisburne. 'I thought you said they were good, Sir Guy. Where is the sport you promised me?' He looked at each of them in turn. 'The great outlaws of Sherwood? I don't see the terrifying warriors that the stories describe. I see a fat monk, a doe-eyed girl, a feckless youth, and… an unthinking thug.'

'You'll pay for that,' Scarlet replied, in a low dangerous voice.

'I think you'll find that today you devalued your currency,' De Baucher said, triumphantly. 'Tie them up.'

As the men-at-arms guarding the outlaws began to bind them, Gisburne noticed that De Baucher had walked over to the village boundary. He warned the Baron that he was making himself a target. 'Hood will worry about the girl, my lord. He'll be watching us.'

'Excellent,' replied Debaucher, 'There *is* sport after all. Sir Guy, take your knife, and cut Hood's woman's throat if an arrow comes my way.'

As Gisburne pulled his blade and held it to Marion's throat, the Baron shouted in the direction of Sherwood. 'In two days,' he said, 'I will return to Wellow and I will hang the captured outlaws. After which, Robin Hood, you and those with you, will then be swiftly hunted down and hanged too.'

He strode back to his horse, which was being brought forwards by one of the soldiers. 'Let's go,' he said to Gisburne, as he mounted up, 'I want to be back in Nottingham by nightfall.'

From their covered position, Robin, Little John and Nasir watched as the convoy began to make its way out of Wellow. All three silently vowed to themselves that no executions would be taking place there in two days from now.

Not every soldier had departed the village, however. One wagon had remained and now the men-at-arms were marshalling the villagers into work groups, overseeing the removal of a large amount of timber from the carts that had arrived with the convoy. There was no delay in the work that was to be carried out before the execution could take place, as the sound of building activity began almost immediately.

'They're making the villagers build something... and I have a nasty suspicion as to what,' commented Robin. 'We need to rest and make a plan, but I want to keep an eye on Wellow too. We'll take it in shifts. I'll take the first watch. You two get some rest; you'll need it.'

John and Nasir moved back into cover, both men wondering if it would be possible to sleep, given what was at stake.

CHAPTER SIX

Dawn, the next day, saw a weary Little John trudge into the camp they had set up close to Wellow. 'You were right, Robin. The soldiers kept the villagers working through the night; they've built a gallows.'

'At least De Baucher didn't surprise us with that,' Robin ruefully replied.

'Could we try getting into Nottingham castle?' asked Little John.

Robin shook his head, 'It will be too well-guarded. Especially if De Baucher's men have taken up residence there.'

Little John, his frustration showing, barked, 'Then what should we *do*? There's no point in us just sitting round a fire and warming our hands. We need to get our hands dirty, Robin!'

Robin looked up, 'What we need, John, is the Sheriff back.'

'I never thought I'd hear you say something like that... or that I would wholeheartedly agree,' said a sombre Little John. 'How though? I mean, for all you know, he could be in the castle dungeon.'

'There *is* someone who will know where he can be found,' Robin replied, 'Abbot Hugo.'

With a sigh, John asked if they were now going to break into the Abbey.

'Breaking in would give the wrong impression,' Robin smirked.

'The *wrong impression?* What do you have in mind, then?' Little John enquired.

'We'll just knock on the door and ask to see him.'

'That will never work!' scoffed Little John. 'I'm telling you, Robin, it's a fool's errand. We'll get cut to ribbons or worse.'

'There' only one way to find out,' Robin stated.

And so it was that Robin and Nasir found themselves approaching the main gate of St. Mary's Abbey.

'John really is going to skulk in the bushes then?' Robin asked.

'He remains in cover, just in case,' Nasir replied with a small smile.

Robin knew that, within minutes, they would find out if Little John's caution was justified. Reaching the gatehouse, the main doors firmly closed, Robin pulled the bell cord. They heard the summoning bell within and shortly after, the approach of footsteps.

A small panel slid back, and the face of a monk appeared, demanding to know who requested entry and for what purpose?

'Robin Hood,' announced Robin, 'I've come to see Abbot Hugo.'

The panel immediately slid shut and, from behind the door, they heard the monk invoking the mercy of the Lord almighty before running off. 'That went well,' said Robin, as they stood there.

'How could you tell?' asked Nasir.

Robin, struggling to explain, soon realised that Nasir was having some fun at his expense.

As they didn't expect anyone to return, they went to walk away from the door, but then heard footsteps approaching again from within. Both men were ready to draw their blades if needs be, but it opened to reveal a monk who—unlike the previous one—was the epitome of disinterested calm. 'The Abbot will see you. You may enter,' he said, as he held the door open for them.

'Thank you, just one moment please,' replied Robin, before shouting back to John that it was safe to come out now. There was a rustling of foliage, and the hairy man mountain emerged, like a passive brown bear, ambling over to join them.

'That shouldn't have worked,' he whispered to Robin.

'Sometimes the best approach is the direct approach,' Robin replied, 'Shall we go in?'

As they did, Little John flipped the smirking Nasir a coin, 'There you are,' he grumbled, 'A wager is a wager.'

The monk led the outlaws through the impressive cloisters that echoed with the distant sound of chanting monks, through to the Abbot's private chapel; the place that Hugo had chosen to see them. 'How do we know that it's not a trap?' asked Little John.

'Because this is a place of worship,' replied the monk indignantly, 'Unless you're expecting us to chant you into submission?' he added dryly.

'Stranger things have happened,' muttered Little John as the door was opened. They were about to enter when the monk looked at Nasir.

'Not him,' he said. Robin was about to protest when Nasir nodded at the monk in acceptance.

'I will wait,' he said calmly. 'To make sure you are truly alone.' It was Robin's turn to nod, then he and Little John went in.

The chapel was beautiful. Small by comparison to other areas of worship within the Abbey, but nonetheless, it took the breath away. At the opposite end to where Robin and Little John had entered, the Sanctuary was bathed in multicoloured sunlight that streamed through a magnificent stained glass window. The calming light spilled onto the sparse pews that were reserved for the Abbot and his guests on which to worship.

Abbot Hugo was standing by a small altar just under the window. When he saw the two outlaws, his face contorted in a snarl as he shouted, 'This is a house of God, wolfshead. How *dare* you bring weapons in here!'

'We have trust issues,' Little John replied.

'I should have you apprehended!' Hugo continued to rage.

'And *that's* why we have trust issues!'

Robin stepped forward to calm the situation, 'My lord Abbot, we are merely here to talk, because I believe we all want the same thing. Namely, the return of your brother to the position of Sheriff, which he appears to have left.'

Hugo bristled, 'My brother never *left* the position! He was forced out. Gisburne and this De Baucher fellow have acted completely outside of their authority. I should have gone to the King!'

'I'm not sure he would be interested,' Robin stated, calmly. 'I think we both know that involving King John isn't a viable option. What if he decides that De Baucher is more worthy of the position your brother held? Isn't it better that this gets sorted quietly, whilst the King focuses on other issues?'

'So, what are you suggesting?' asked Hugo, slowly calming down throughout Robin's sensible explanation.

'I'm suggesting we co-operate,' Robin replied. 'Help us to help you. It can't have been pleasant having Gisburne lord it over you.'

Hugo looked rattled. He couldn't quite believe that he was having this conversation. 'Even if I *do* decide to help,' he said, 'there is a problem. The one that started these strange events off in the first place.'

'What do you mean?'

'I will show you,' Hugo said. 'But *only* you, Hood. Your heathen of a henchman can stay here or join his filthy Arab friend outside the door.'

'Isn't the Church such a welcoming, compassionate place?' muttered Little John, under his breath.

'What did he say?' barked Hugo.

'He says he understands,' Robin lied, shooting Little John an 'I'm sorry' type of look, as he began to follow Abbot Hugo.

The Abbey's gardens were the epitome of tranquillity itself; part ornamental, landscaped as a retreat for the brothers to enjoy and use as a place of contemplation, part land that was worked to provide fresh produce for the community within the walls to consume (on top of that supplied by the people of the shire).

As gentle birdsong filled the air, Robin and the Abbot walked their way along a dirt track that ran through the various allotments; allotments that were being lovingly tilled by the brothers... and one other figure that Robin only recognised as they got closer. 'That man working the earth, it isn't..?' His question died in disbelief at what he was seeing.

As Hugo hurried on, in front of Robin, he shouted out. 'Robert, you can stop that for a moment! You have a visitor!'

The Sheriff looked up, blinking in the sun, and wiped the sweat from his brow with a soil-encrusted forearm. As soon as he saw who it was that had come to see him, he face broke into a smile and he dropping his hoe, stepping forwards to embrace Robin as if he were a long lost brother.

'Um... my lord...' managed Robin, clearly taken aback as he disentangled himself from the man who—at one time—he would have considered to be his arch enemy.

'Call me Robert, please; you must call me Robert,' said De Rainault with genuine warmth, before adding, 'I owe you an apology.'

'There's no need,' Robin said awkwardly

'No need at all,' Hugo added, agreeing with Robin.

But De Rainault insisted there was. 'You see Robert, I can't remember what we were fighting about. When the people are happy, life is so much better. For everyone!'

Robin couldn't believe that this sentiment was real, that these words were coming from the Sheriff's own lips, and he had to take a moment to breathe it in.

The Sheriff went on. 'The apology is freely given. I should have done it earlier. And a free pardon, for you and all of your men, of course!'

'Steady now, Robert!' Hugo exclaimed.

'That's very gracious of you, my lord Sheriff,' said Robin, 'but I need the opposite of a pardon. It's that lack of fight between us that I need to talk about with you.'

'I don't understand?'

'The people are suffering.'

'Oh dear. Because you and I are not at loggerheads? That seems very odd. However, I am only just learning the whims and quirks of the people over whom I governed for so long. What can I do to help?' asked the concerned Sheriff.

'They need you back,' Robin stated. If these were words that Robin never dreamed he would have cause to say, then the Sheriff's reply was even more surprising.

'There was a time when all I craved was power, but that was before I found this.'

'My lord?' Robin questioned.

'These gardens. These vegetables. The calm serenity of it. All I crave now is to till the soil and be at peace.'

'And you can be, Robert, but not by wallowing in this filth and mud,' snapped Hugo.

'But without this mud—*your* mud, Hugo— where would the food come from that we eat? I have finally found my vocation!' said the Sheriff contentedly.

The Abbot had just about had enough of this and exploded with pent-up frustration. 'Take a look at yourself, brother!' he snapped, 'Your fine clothes, made from the best material, now dirt-encrusted and in tatters. And for a man so fond of bathing, you've not washed once since you've been here. It's not right!'

As Hugo simmered, Robin quietly agreed. 'My lord Sheriff, it would be better for everyone if you were able to clean yourself up and return to your position, especially if you genuinely want to help the people of Nottinghamshire.'

De Rainault now looked sadly at the two men, sworn enemies brought together by their desire to have *his* help. Despite his new-found status as a unifying force, he wasn't sure that he wanted to go back to being the Sheriff. 'The people hated me,' he reflected.

'They will hate you even more if you don't help.'

'Why?' asked the Sheriff, feeling instantly sad.

'I'm afraid De Baucher and Gisburne are running a brutal regime,' said Robin. 'But when the people hear what you have done to save them, they'll love you even more. You have a power right now that no one else has.'

'More power than I ever craved. Hah. I think that's sadly ironic, because I don't want it,' the Sheriff replied.

Once more, Robin pleaded with his former enemy. 'The people would want you to use this new power.'

Again, De Rainault was reticent. 'Power corrupts.'

'Now you know that,' Robin pointed out, 'you'll use it wisely.'

The Sheriff considered for a few moments and turned his face to the sun, soaking up the rays before turning his attention back to Robin. 'You could help me,' he said, 'Together, we could build a new shire!' In that moment, as the two men took each others' hands, forging a new friendship, the mood was soured by the Abbot.

'This is all very… *laudable,* but how will you achieve this utopian dream? De Baucher and Gisburne run things now.'

Fortunately, Robin had a few thoughts about that. 'The Sheriff will return to his rightful position with a victory that simply cannot be matched or ignored. He will do something that would ensure his authority.'

'And what would that be?' asked Hugo.

'The capture of Robin Hood!' came Robin's reply.

CHAPTER SEVEN

The combination of the fire that roared in the hearth of the great hall, and the wine he was consuming, warmed De Baucher, but not enough. It was never enough. He took another gulp as Gisburne walked in. He poured the younger man a goblet, which was readily accepted.

'Everything seems to be proceeding smoothly, my lord,' Sir Guy reported.

De Baucher gave an absent nod and looked into the flames, 'I think, as the men are not here, we can dispense with the formalities. Please continue, Guy.'

'All of our wagons have returned fully laden; the tithes and the additional supplies as ordered. We have also recovered most of the gold that the Sheriff, I mean the *previous* sheriff, gave away.'

'But not the money stolen by Robin Hood?' De Baucher asked.

'I'm afraid not,' Gisburne replied.

De Baucher knew that if it were hidden in Sherwood, it would be impossible to find, unless they first captured Robin and made him talk. The whole operation could be a huge drain on resources, but he had come up with a strategy to deal with the ever-present threat the outlaws posed. He said as much to Gisburne, who took a sip of his wine and settled back in a chair, eager to hear the plan.

De Baucher was willing to write off the stolen money in return for a guaranteed victory over not just Robin Hood, but any and all fugitives who sought refuge in Sherwood. A victory that would see a permanent end to the forest being considered a safe haven.

By now, Gisburne was most intrigued. Taking another gulp of wine and gazing into the fire, De Baucher casually outlined his thinking, 'To do this, I intend to burn Sherwood to the ground.'

Gisburne spat his wine out with the shock of what he heard, the fine red mist caught in the light of the fire. Again, De Baucher didn't look away from the flames, 'You really shouldn't waste the wine, Guy; it's a very good and very costly vintage.'

Gisburne wiped his mouth on his sleeve. 'Surely this is some form of joke?' he queried.

'No, I am quite serious,' returned De Baucher, 'I intend to burn it all to the ground. Every last tree. Don't you see, it is the only way. A cleansing fire to extinguish the outlaw plague.'

'Sherwood is a *royal* forest! The King... well... he will no doubt have something to say about the matter,' Gisburne replied desperately.

'That's true. He will exult us,' De Baucher replied.

'The King?' questioned Gisburne.

'It was he who came to me with this plan, and we will revel in his rapture,' De Baucher revealed.

Gisburne was now worried, but De Baucher continued. 'When the trees burn, the power of Robin Hood will be wiped out.'

'But there are the countless villages in and around the forest, William. *They'll* burn as well,' Gisburne said, trying to reason with his friend.

De Baucher replied, far too calmly, 'In war, Guy, casualties must be expected. I really didn't think that *you* would be so squeamish about the idea of a few peasant deaths.'

'It's not only peasants,' Gisburne countered, 'It's the King's timber, his property. That has always been made very clear to me by the Sheriff...'

At this, De Baucher exploded and launched himself at Gisburne, the speed of the assault taking the young knight by surprise. His hands were now at Gisburne's throat. 'THE SHERIFF? *I AM THE SHERIFF!*' De Baucher shouted into Gisburne's shocked face. 'Let me make things clear to you, Guy, I am proposing the biggest single victory this shire will ever see: the destruction of Robin Hood! And all you can worry about is timber? Who is Robin Hood to you anyway?'

Gisburne now felt genuine fear as the Baron outlined why his proposed plan was the only way. 'The action I will take is extreme but necessary for the safety of everything we hold dear.'

'But *surely* there has to be another way, William?' Gisburne gasped, risking another round of rage.

As expected, a fury took hold of De Baucher as he screamed at Sir Guy to address him with the proper courtesy now. 'I'm sorry, *my lord,*' Gisburne stammered. Then, in the next instant, a calm seemed to descend upon De Baucher as he looked kindly upon his shaken comrade. 'Wait, I can see it now,' he whispered in Gisburne's ear, 'You are weak and not up to the task of doing what must be done. We are not on the same journey.'

'That is not true, my lord!' Gisburne spluttered.

The Baron looked at his former friend, and pinned him against the hearth, the heat maddeningly painful. 'Remember what I said before,' De Baucher hissed, 'Those who were not with me, are against me.'

De Baucher's grip around Gisburne's throat was like iron, and—through gulps of snatched air—he pleaded to be permitted to prove himself the loyal ally that he was... but the Baron had already called for his guards.

The doors to the hall were flung open and the Baron's soldiers presented themselves at their master's call. 'Arrest Sir Guy!' De Baucher ordered as he released his grip on Gisburne's neck. Gisburne gasped great gulps of air as his legs turned to jelly and he collapsed on to his knees.

'*You* of all people, Guy,' De Baucher sighed, sadly.

The guards yanked him up off the straw that covered the flagstones, and—having regained his breath properly—Gisburne protested. 'William, this is ridiculous!' he cried. 'You men, release me this instant and take *this* man into custody, not me,' Gisburne pleaded, but the guards were not his and they ignored his plea.

De Baucher had a silky-smooth richness to his voice as he spoke without feeling, 'The penalty for treason is death. You're nothing but a criminal now. As such, you will hang with the outlaws.'

'No!' uttered Gisburne, astonished by the callousness of the man he had recently considered a friend.

'Guards, you can put Sir Guy into the dungeon with the outlaws. Before they meet their end, they might enjoy a few hours of revenge on their foe.'

'This is insane,' Gisburne muttered, as his energy dipped from struggling so hard in the grip of the guards.

'Oh, but don't let the prisoners kill him. Keep watch. They can harm him as much as they like, but we wouldn't want Sir Guy to cheat tomorrow's hanging noose.'

He dismissed the guards with a wave of his hand, and they dragged a squirming and grunting Gisburne from the hall, the doors slamming shut after they had left.

CHAPTER EIGHT

The next day had seen an early start for De Baucher and his captives, who were unceremoniously awoken by being drenched, the castle guards hurling buckets of freezing water down into the dank pit that was used as the castle dungeon.

And now they found themselves standing in Wellow village, with a freshly constructed gallows ominously waiting for them.

De Baucher ordered that the outlaws and Sir Guy be put onto the structure.

Gisburne was shoved and pushed along with Tuck, Much, Scarlet and Marion onto the wooden platform. The men-at-arms tied their hands behind them and then placed a noose around each of their necks. It was all becoming very real.

De Baucher then had his soldiers corral the villagers into the square so that they might witness his actions. He strode out to address them. 'People of Wellow, today you witness the beginning of the end for those who would challenge my authority.'

He then took a few steps to the boundary of the village and addressed Sherwood, sure that his nemesis would be watching.

'Robin Hood, do not feel any grief for your friends; you will not be parted from them for long. Death will soon re-unite you.'

He then walked back to the gallows. He wanted to wait before he gave the command that would see his prisoners hang. He wanted to feel their fear and draw out the agony.

During the time that the captured outlaws were making their way into Wellow, within a clearing inside Sherwood that allowed a view through to the village, Robin, Little John and Nasir were with the De Rainault brothers.

Robin, along with the De Rainaults, was mounted, something that would aid them considerably in getting to Wellow in time to save their friends. He turned to the Sheriff and asked if he was ready.

The Sheriff had a question, 'How did I act before, exactly? I've forgotten.'

'You were angry.' Hugo replied.

'Yes,' Robin agreed.

'Sarcastic,' continued Hugo, before adding, 'Cynical. Sharp-tongued. Egotistical. With a total and utter lack of empathy.'

'Yes, thank you, Hugo,' said the Sheriff, 'I think I get it. But, if I was all of those things, how did they mesh together into one? How did I put that all together?'

Robin tried his best at a rough approximation of an impression, 'Sort of like, "GISBURNE! I would ask what you were thinking, but you clearly don't think. Fetch me a jug of wine, you dimwit!"—does that ring any bells?'

There was a silence, as the Sheriff took this in. 'Ah yes,' he said, 'like this… "GISBUUUUURNE!"'

'Welcome back, brother!' said a relieved Hugo.

Little John now pressed Robin on the time that was fast running out. They edged closer to the tree line to see their captured friends being frog-marched towards the scaffold. It was then that Little John noticed there was an extra person with them: to his surprise, Gisburne was also included in the prisoner party. He pointed this out to the group.

'What?' said a shocked Robin. It was now that Herne's prophecy echoed within his mind. *A destiny awaits you. It would see you save one who is bound to you by blood, and is yet a stranger to you, divided from you by that same blood.* Robin also heard his reply as it came back to haunt him. 'You make it sound like there isn't a choice.'

'If you value those close to you, there is not,' Herne had replied.

Dragging himself back into the moment, Robin reflected that he hadn't trodden carefully enough in trying to choose a new path. But now, it was time they were moving.

As they did, the Sheriff caught sight of his steward. 'Guy looks in rather a sorry state,' he commented, and it was true. Gisburne's time with the outlaws had not been harmonious. De Rainault continued. 'No offence, Robin, but I can certainly understand why your men are there, but why Guy?'

Hugo had the answer. 'It's Gisburne, Robert, there are *plenty* of reasons why he's up there. I've been tempted to hang him myself a few times.'

'Maybe if you had, we all wouldn't be here now,' Little John said grimly.

Calming everyone down and instructing Little John and Nasir to stay back and act as cover, Robin urged his horse forwards, and rode out with the Abbot and with the Sheriff.

A soft wind blew through Wellow, which lay in the throes of a terrible enforced silence. The occasional movement of a soldier's horse broke the mute soundtrack to the scene that was being played out in the village square, that of the outlaws and Sir Guy of Gisburne, all standing on the gallows that had been constructed specifically for them.

De Baucher, having savoured the atmosphere for long enough, was now preparing to carry out his promise to hang them all.

On the wooden platform, Marion whispered a prayer for Robin's appearance. Gisburne muttered that her faith was misplaced. Tuck now broke off from his own silent contemplations to remind the knight that faith was never misplaced. Even in the face of death, Gisburne wasn't going to let his enemy have the final word. 'Oh? Just look at what's happened. De Baucher has beaten us all. Hood would be better looking to himself, rather than bothering to try and save us.'

'You're not part of "us", Gisburne,' Scarlet hissed. 'It's *us* that he'll be coming to save, not you.'

Gisburne shrugged, 'It's a battle he can't win. If I were him…'

Marion cut Gisburne off. 'You're *not* him. Not even close.'

'You could have been,' Tuck muttered, to himself more than anything.

Sir Guy, overhearing the remark, demanded to know what Friar Tuck meant. He was deflected from pursuing the line of questioning further by Much, who was pointing out that De Baucher was about to give the final command. They were surely about to die.

It was then that they saw the horses galloping into the village and a familiar voice rang out as Robert de Rainault cried 'STOP! Stop in the name of the King!'

'I *knew* it!' exclaimed Marion.

'We *all* did, Little Flower,' Tuck replied as he sent a silent prayer of thanks to the almighty. It was Much who articulated what they were all wondering. 'Why is Robin with the Sheriff?'

They were about to find out.

A furious De Baucher strode over and demanded an explanation for the interruption, as well as the sudden reappearance of the De Rainault brothers. 'What do you think you are doing?' he yelled.

'I could, in fact I will, ask *you* the same question,' the Sheriff said calmly. De Baucher, now a mixture of anger and exasperation, answered in clipped tones.

'You can see plainly what I'm doing. You, on the other hand, have just ridden here in the company of a known criminal.'

'Yes, and I will take it from here,' the Sheriff replied, again his calm demeanour a stark contrast to De Baucher's, who was becoming even more agitated.

'You're in no fit state to.'

'Really? Then Robin Hood *isn't* my prisoner?' mocked De Rainault, playing his trump card.

De Baucher shot a questioning look at Robin, who was only too happy to confirm that he had indeed surrendered to the Sheriff. De Baucher seized on this admission and yelled out 'Then we must put him on the scaffold too! Guards!'

As the soldiers stepped forwards, Abbot Hugo bellowed at them. 'If any of you make a move against Robin, or anyone connected to him or the

Sheriff, then you and your entire families will be excommunicated from the church.'

At this, not one single man-at-arms moved a step further.

De Baucher began to rant that De Rainault was not in charge. Still a picture of serenity, the Sheriff replied. 'I think you'll find that we're more in control than you are.'

Moving forwards on his horse, the Sheriff addressed the soldiers directly. 'Now, you men, listen to me. The King never sanctioned transfer of power. I am your rightful Sheriff, and in the name of the King, I am assuming command. Unless of course, you'd like to take this up with his majesty, De Baucher?'

De Baucher didn't reply immediately, but when he did, his words conveyed another meaning altogether. 'Perhaps I will go to seek an audience with His Highness. He will provide me with more power than you have ever dreamt of. He will not fail me!' Yet recognising that, in this moment, he could not win, De Baucher called his men to his side, mounted up and—together with his soldiers— galloped out of Wellow.

As De Baucher and his men swept past him and out of the village, the Sheriff asked where the captain of the castle guard was. He stepped forwards, 'I'm here,' he said. The Sheriff looked at him.

'Here?' he questioned. *'Here?* I think we're forgetting something, aren't we?'

The captain remembered his station immediately and bowed before his lord. 'I am here, *my lord.'*

'That's better!' praised the returning Sheriff, 'Now, I need you to return the tithes and taxes taken by De Baucher illegally, back to the people he collected them from.'

Clearly at a loss, the captain then blurted out that they were stored in Nottingham, whilst he and his men were here in Wellow.

'Then you had better get moving,' the Sheriff replied curtly.

'My lord, surely you can't mean that?' asked the captain.

'Are you trying to suggest that I'm somehow jesting with you? Have you ever known me to enjoy a good joke?'

It was Robin's turn to pitch in. He threw a bag of money onto the ground. The same money that he had originally stolen from the Sheriff and had had so much trouble returning to the people. It was to be added to what was going to be given back.

The Captain hesitated, clearly mystified by

the Sheriff's behaviour, but now too scared to face the consequences if he questioned his orders any further. Picking up the money, he ordered his men to mount up.

As the soldiers departed, Robin called for Nasir and Little John, who strolled into the village. 'It's time to get everyone off the gallows, if you two would do the honours?'

'What of Gisburne?' asked Nasir.

'Him as well,' Robin replied. He turned to the Sheriff, still mounted on his horse beside him. 'Congratulations on a vintage performance, my lord!'

'I think it did the trick,' Robert De Rainault said cheerfully.

'Yes, very convincing,' muttered Abbot Hugo, snidely. 'But now what?' asked Abbot Hugo. The others all looked at Robin.

'Now I think we need to give you an escort through Sherwood,' he said. 'Together as friends.'

CHAPTER NINE

Will Scarlet was not a happy man and was making his disapproval of the current alliance between the outlaws and the De Rainault brothers very clear to Little John. 'I'm telling ya, this ain't right.'

'Why isn't it?' asked Little John, 'We won, eh Tuck?'

'It certainly looks like it,' Friar Tuck agreed.

Frustrated that his comrades clearly felt differently about the situation, Scarlet now approached Marion. 'You 'ave to 'ave a word with Robin. First chance they get, this will go bad, and you know it.'

'All I know is that Robin believes in this, so it's good enough for me,' she replied, before adding, 'for now.'

Scarlet wasn't the only one with misgivings. Gisburne was trying his best to appeal to Abbot Hugo. 'You can't sanction this, my lord Abbot. The Sheriff is clearly still affected. Just look at his behaviour.'

'You are in no position to talk about behaviour, Gisburne,' the Abbot replied.

'Are you telling me you're comfortable walking with the outlaws?'

Abbot Hugo didn't answer. It was a silent pause that was fertile enough for Gisburne to start sowing in the seeds of doubt. 'The first chance they get, they will kill us without mercy, my lord Abbot.'

The Abbot still stayed silent, his eyes darting back and forth to each outlaw around him, and his logical mind spinning.

As the procession made its way through Sherwood, the Sheriff and Robin walked side by side, as if they were old friends. 'I do mean it about the pardon I can grant you and your friends,' De Rainault reiterated, 'It wasn't an empty promise.'

'Thank you. That is much appreciated. I think it would arouse the King's suspicion too much, sadly.'

The Sheriff nodded, he understood that it might seem odd that he was asking for a pardon from a band of rebels who'd been nothing but a thorn in his side for years now. He became reflective for a moment, as he glanced back at his steward. 'What to do with Gisburne, though?' he pondered. 'I'm afraid he will never accept the situation. It's always difficult when you suddenly cease to be an only child, if you'll pardon the metaphor.'

'Um... quite,' said Robin, the implications of the Sheriff's words not lost on him.

There was a crack of thunder, rumbling from above. As Robin looked up, he saw that the sky was darkening. The air was also becoming colder. The storm appeared to have developed from nowhere, as if the elements had suddenly somehow been manipulated.

Then they heard it.

The unmistakable sound of men charging into battle.

As an unnatural storm began to tear the sky apart, and a fierce wind began to blow, Robin could now see their assailants; it was De Baucher and his men, charging in on horseback.

As Robin told the Sheriff and Hugo to get into cover—the Sheriff urging his horse on and Hugo doing the same—he dismounted and, together with the others, prepared to defend themselves against the oncoming charge. Bows at the ready, they felled the first wave of soldiers with a volley of arrows, but the second wave saw the outlaws engaged in close combat.

De Baucher's soldiers began to fight the outlaws, but it quickly became apparent that—for all their advantages of horses and numbers—these were men who were inexperienced in the harsh realities of close-quarter combat.

Ignoring the fact that his men were a diminished force as they were felled from their mounts by arrow or outlaw, through the carnage De Baucher was walking, looking for his quarry. He found him quickly. 'Do you see now that we are at war, Guy?' he cried at Gisburne. 'Now you will face me!'

'Look at yourself!' cried Gisburne, 'Whatever has possessed you, William!' he added, not recognizing his friend anymore, even though the shell of the man looked the same as he'd always done.

'How interesting you should put it like that. Look at *yourself*, Guy. Consorting with the enemy as if you were brothers...' De Baucher then launched himself at Gisburne.

The ferocity of the attack and the skill that De Baucher showed with his sword soon had Sir Guy on the back foot. One moment later, after losing his balance, he was sprawled in the dust. De Baucher's full attention was now focused on Gisburne, so much so that he didn't even realise that the battle was over, and his men had lost.

De Baucher raised his sword and brought it down to deliver a killing blow to Gisburne. Yet it never came as his blade was blocked by Albion. De Baucher looked up at Robin. If he had been prevented from finishing the job, it was but a pleasure deferred. *Here was more sport,* he thought as he turned his attack on Robin.

As they battled, the wind continued to blow and lightning continued to strike, intensifying with each clash of their swords.

Struggling to know how to intervene without the distraction affecting Robin, the outlaws witnessed the power that De Baucher wielded. 'This can't be normal,' Marion said, straining to raise her voice above the swirling storm. 'We have to stop it somehow!'

For all of De Baucher's inhuman strength and ability, Robin's skill with Albion was keeping him at bay. De Baucher pulled away from Robin, and in the moment that he took to catch his breath, Gisburne had moved to Robin's side, sword in hand.

'Gisburne's attacking! Come on!' shouted Will Scarlet, but his path to them was blocked momentarily by the bulk of Friar Tuck.

'No,' the man of God said, placing a hand on Scarlet's chest to stop him coming forward, 'They have to finish this, Robin and Gisburne, together,' Tuck said firmly.

'But Tuck!' Scarlet growled.

'Trust me. They are fighting together, not apart. It's the blood that binds.'

In a further series of thrust and parry, De Baucher took on the two blades and it became a whirling dervish of a dance. When it looked like Robin and Gisburne had got the upper hand, De Baucher would came back stronger. When it looked like De Baucher might finally have one of them, the other would step in and prevent the final blow.

The rain started to pelt down, and the forest floor became more and more slippery. In a final surge, De Baucher's sword found Gisburne, as he briefly lost his footing, slicing through the knight's arm and causing him to spin away from the fight in pain.

A lightening bolt hit a tree nearby, and the crack of the collision between electricity and wood caused an explosion of sparks and illuminated the trunk.

It was one on one, and Robin, being pushed back, suddenly found himself stumbling over a fallen branch that had sheared off the tree that had been struck. It was only the smallest of stumbles, but it coincided with a vicious blow that De Baucher rained on Albion, and Robin tumbled down onto the hard surface of the forest road.

De Baucher could taste his victory as he stepped forwards, flames licking high in the air from the tree that had connected with the sky. 'Time for a new story to be written,' he snarled, his teeth seemingly stuck together and his top lip curled upwards, like a rabid dog. 'They will write about how you died at my hand whilst you crawled in the dust!' he spat.

'ROBIN!' Marion cried as she tried to run to him, but again Friar Tuck held her, and the others, at bay.

'Keep back, all of you!' he said. 'It's up to them now!'

As De Baucher brought his sword down for the killing blow, the blade rang out as it met, not flesh, but Sir Guy of Gisburne's sword. He'd crawled towards the fight and used all the power he could to hold his sword steady, his stronger arm bleeding profusely from De Baucher's wounding of him. 'I can't block him for long!' Gisburne cried out, 'Finish it, Robert of Huntingdon!'

The mention of his true name sent a surge of strength through Robin and he pulled his sword,

Albion, up from the floor and ran De Baucher through. There was a look of puzzlement on De Baucher's face, one that soon turned to something like understanding. As Robin pulled his blade free, the bleeding baron looked at his opponents.

'Oh... how strange not to have seen it earlier...' he opined, 'but, in that moment between the light and the dark, my master has shown me what you are to each other.'

He then turned his head to the sky and cried out, 'Oh my King of the world, I have failed thee!'

The sky again crackled with lightning, and the thunder seemed to shake the very earth beneath their feet, as the wind whipped up the dust and the leaves all around them.

In the next moment, William De Baucher seemed to implode, and as his body crumpled. On the wind, it seemed to Gisburne that a spectral voice called his name out, calling him to ride with them.

We are legion, it said. Then it was gone in a flash.

As the dust settled and the storm subsided, Marion turned to Tuck, 'What—What was that?'

'Faith being answered,' was the Friar's reply.

Gisburne was now helping Robin to his feet. 'You saved my life. Thank you,' Robin uttered.

'You did the same for me,' Gisburne replied.

'Guy, there's something you need to be told,' Robin began, but he was interrupted by Will Scarlet tapping Gisburne on the shoulder. As he turned, Scarlet landed a terrific punch and the steward collapsed out cold onto the road.

Robin was furious. Calling Friar Tuck over to look at the prone form of Sir Guy to see if he was okay, he rounded on Scarlet, demanding an explanation as to why he had behaved in such a way.

'Why? *Why?*' Scarlet shouted, 'Because this isn't normal, that's why!'

A rustling of wet foliage signalled the return of the Sheriff and the Abbot, emerging from their hiding place, both having had to abandon their mounts as they became increasingly spooked by the storm that had torn across the sky. 'Thank the Maker you're all alive, especially you, Robert of Huntingdon. Let me embrace you as a comrade!'

As he began to approach, Robin saw that the lightning-scorched tree, weakened by the forces that had torn De Baucher apart at the end, was beginning to topple... and De Rainault was right in its path!

He ran forwards and, as the tree crashed, he pushed the Sheriff out of the way. As he fell, though, De Rainault hit the ground hard and his head cracked loudly against the road surface.

Both Robin and Hugo were at the Sheriff's side in a split second, Robin gently trying to rouse the unconscious form. Hugo, as ungracious as ever, pushed Robin away. 'Leave him alone! *I* shall tend to my brother!'

Knowing when he wasn't welcome, Robin walked over to the others. 'I did my best,' he said, adding, 'At least he isn't laying under a fallen tree!'

'It was an accident. Just a freak accident. You weren't too know he'd hit his head,' said Marion, trying her best to comfort him.

Just then, there was a stirring from the fallen Sheriff. 'He's coming round…' cried Hugo excitedly. 'Robert… Robert, do you know who I am?'

'Of course I know who you are, Hugo!' snapped the Sheriff, 'Only *you* could be so annoying as to ask such a redundant question.'

Abbot Hugo, an uncharacteristic smile playing on his lips, then asked the Sheriff what he remembered. Puzzled by the question, De Rainault looked around him and demanded to know what his brother was doing in Sherwood forest and why he lay in the sodden dirt.

Robert persisted with his questions, 'And why do I have a pounding headache? Have we been drinking, Hugo?'

'No, no we weren't drinking,' said Hugo, 'but this is going to sound like we have been. Do you happen to remember cultivating vegetables at all?' he asked.

'The only vegetable I remember cultivating is Gisburne. Now where is he?' questioned the Sheriff, now very irritable indeed.

'You're back, brother!' cried a delighted Hugo.

'Yes,' De Rainault replied, 'My back, my front, my sides, my everything... all in great pain as I lay on Sherwood Forest's floor. What does this *mean*, Hugo? Where's Gisburne?'

Hugo pointed to the unconscious figure lying on the road, a bit further down from him.

'Have we all suffered from a sleeping sickness?' mocked the Sheriff. 'Don't tell me we decided to all have a little camping trip in Sherwood? We clearly *have* been drinking...'

The Sheriff's eyes widened to their fullest extent, as Robin Hood walked forwards into his line of vision.

'Of course!' cried the Sheriff, recalling the moments before Much had hit him with a slingshot and he'd first bashed his head on the ground, 'You ambushed us! But, no, wait... I don't recall Hugo being here, that was not how it happened.' He shook his head to try and clear the dull throb, and his eyes focused on the rest of the outlaws nearby. 'It matters not, though, clearly. If the outlaws are going to kill us, Hugo, then they had better get on with it! I'm fed up of being soggy, muddy and dizzy!'

Will Scarlet didn't need telling twice and had pulled his blade free when Robin firmly told him to stop. Scarlet frowned and put the blade back in its sheath. Robin looked at the Sheriff, with sorrow etched across his face. 'I'm so sorry, Sheriff.'

'I don't need your pity. Do it,' De Rainault cried.

'I don't think so. There's been enough killing for one day. Wouldn't you agree, Hugo?' Robin asked.

'That's *Abbot* Hugo to you, wolfshead!' came the clipped reply.

'I have a feeling that you're going to be much more use to me alive. Goodbye, Abbot. Goodbye, Sheriff. It was nice to get to know you properly.'

Robin rejoined the others and led them away with a simple, 'Let's go.'

EPILOGUE

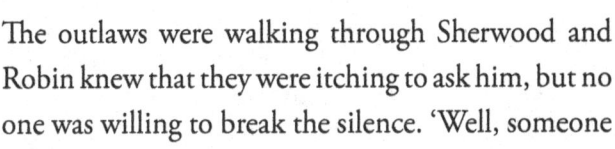

The outlaws were walking through Sherwood and Robin knew that they were itching to ask him, but no one was willing to break the silence. 'Well, someone ask me then. I know you want to,' he finally said.

'Alright,' Marion replied. 'I will. Why did you save the Sheriff?'

'Yeah, especially as he seemed worse than ever,' said Much.

'We could have solved a big problem, Robin,' Little John said.

'Have you gone soft in the head?' asked the characteristically blunt Scarlet.

'Nasir, what do you think?' asked Robin.

'I do not think you are soft. But mercy always comes at a price.'

Finally, Friar Tuck had his say. 'I know why you didn't kill the Sheriff. Go on, tell them,' he prompted Robin.

'We've just had a taste of what could happen if the Sheriff is ever gone. And it's *worse* than if he stays in power. After all, we know we can beat *this* Sheriff, and—'

Friar Tuck interrupted, to finish the sentence, '—and it's better the devil you know. In more ways than one!'

Also from Chinbeard and Oak Tree Books...

You may also enjoy...

Richard Carpenter's
ROBIN OF
SHERWOOD

THE
HUNTRESS

Jennifer Ash